THE INTERNET LIBRARY

Creating E-Reports and Online Presentations

Gerry, Janet, and Allison Souter

Enslow Publishers, Inc.

40 Industrial Road	PO Box 38
Box 398	Aldershot
Berkeley Heights, NJ 07922	Hants GU12 6BP
USA	UK

http://www.enslow.com

Books in THE INTERNET LIBRARY series

Bringing Photos, Music, and Video
Into Your Web Page
ISBN 0-7660-2082-7

Communicating on the Internet
ISBN 0-7660-1260-3

Creating and Publishing
Web Pages on the Internet
ISBN 0-7660-1262-X

Creating Animation for Your Web Page
ISBN 0-7660-2083-5

Creating E-Reports and
Online Presentations
ISBN 0-7660-2080-0

The History of the Internet
and the World Wide Web
ISBN 0-7660-1261-1

Internet Power Research Using
the Big6™ Approach
ISBN 0-7660-2094-0

Locating and Evaluating
Information on the Internet
ISBN 0-7660-1259-X

Researching on the Internet Using
Search Engines, Bulletin Boards,
and Listservs
ISBN 0-7660-2081-9

Safe Surfing on the Internet
ISBN 0-7660-2030-4

Copyright © 2003 by Enslow Publishers, Inc.

All rights reserved.

No part of this book may be reproduced by any means
without the written permission of the publisher.

Library of Congress Cataloging-in-Publication Data

Souter, Gerry.
    Creating E-reports and online presentations / by Gerry, Janet, and
    Allison Souter.
        v. cm. — (The Internet library)
        Contents: How to begin your report — Adding visuals to your web
    report— Creating graphics for your report — Laying out your web report
    —Creating your report in HTML.
        ISBN 0-7660-2080-0
        1. Web sites—Design—Juvenile literature. 2. Report writing—
    Juvenile literature. [1. Web sites—Design. 2. Report writing.] I. Souter,
    Janet, 1940– II. Souter, Allison. III. Title. IV. Series.
    TK5205.888.S67 2003
    005.7'2—dc21   2002155844

Printed in the United States of America

10 9 8 7 6 5 4 3 2 1

To Our Readers:
We have done our best to make sure all Internet addresses in this book were
active and appropriate when we went to press. However, the author and the
publisher have no control over and assume no liability for the material
available on those Internet sites or on other Web sites they may link to. Any
comments or suggestions can be sent by e-mail to comments@enslow.com
or to the address on the back cover.

Trademarks:
Most computer and software brand names have trademarks or registered
trademarks. The individual trademarks have not been listed here.

Cover Photo: ©Index Stock Imagery, Eric Kamp

Contents

Introduction

This is my friend Web. He will be appearing throughout the pages of this book to guide you through the information presented here and to take you to a variety of Internet sites and activities. Web is also a reminder that there is always more to learn about the Internet.

Come along with us and Web to discover how to create a report on the World Wide Web. This report will be a far cry from the run-of-the-mill three pages of scribbled-on notebook paper. This report is going to rock!

Just about everybody has to write a report sometime to tell about a job completed, describe a project, or give information to people who need it. Making a report is a real-life skill you will need in any career you choose.

The neat thing is, today you can do so much more than just sit down and write until your hand hurts. Today, you can create reports on the Web. They can include words, photographs, drawings, animations, charts, even video. They are actually a lot of fun, especially if you are creative.

A Web report allows you to show, not just tell. You do this by using what we call graphics. These include photographs, drawings, animations, maps, and charts, such as graphs and tables. The graphics

Internet Addresses   Communication Facts   How Can I Be Safe?

Before we start, you might want to ask, "Why do we have to write reports in school anyway?" You write reports to learn a number of very useful skills:

1. How to organize your thoughts

2. How to create an outline

3. How to use different research techniques

4. How to tell an interesting and accurate story

can be put right on the page, or they can be designed to come up when the viewer clicks on a "hot" word. For instance, maps can be created that allow the viewer to "zoom in" on a location.

Keep in mind that a Web report has an international audience. People in Paris, Beijing, Mexico City, or Big Timber, Montana, can appreciate your work. Since there might be a million or so visitors to your site, you might want to ask yourself the following questions:

Text and Graphics:
The word *text* refers to the words you write for the report. The graphics are the pictures and charts—all the visual things.

- What browsers might your visitors be using? Internet Explorer? Netscape? You want to set the report up so that the maximum number of people can view all your storytelling elements, including things like video clips and scrolling text.

- Will people need those special programs attached to their browsers called "plug-ins," such as Flash, RealAudio, and RealVideo?

• Will the connection speed of most modems permit downloading your files, viewing streaming video, listening to audio files, or seeing an animation the way you created it?

We'll show you how to manage all these report elements without feeling like a juggler with too many balls in the air. Besides all that, we'll also discuss *aesthetics*. This word refers to the beauty, or artistry, of the report. Think of a Web page as a painter's canvas rather than a piece of lined notebook paper. A good Web report uses different fonts (type styles), colors, and graphics, without being too fussy and confusing. Aesthetics is about creating a solid report that is also attractive to look at.

In the chapters that follow, we'll take advantage of many Web tools to create a great report, but first we need a subject. Imagine your teacher asking for a report on "events that changed Earth's environment." Since we want to create a report that "rocks," let's look at the spectacular exploders that created so many actual rocks. We'll do a report on fire-belching, lava-drooling, gas-passing volcanoes! You'll even get to see this amazing report when it's finished, because an image of the Web page we created appears on page 56. The code we used is all written out in the appendix, which begins on page 57. Feel free to use your own modified version of the code to create a Web masterpiece.

Turn on your brain, grab your mouse, and hang on as we begin to make a report that tells a billion-year-old story about the volcanoes that are still violently shaping Earth today.

Chapter 1

How to Begin Your Report

hether you are creating an electronic report on the Web or writing one out on paper, there are steps you can take to make sure your research goes smoothly and the result turns out well. Here, we'll talk about choosing a topic, getting organized, and planning your time.

A report has one major purpose: to provide information. You might use lots of fancy things to make it more fun, such as pictures, sound, charts, and video, but the main thing has to be the explanation of your subject. Why did the bridge collapse? How did the war start? What makes a volcano erupt? Where do whales live?

A good report uses language that is simple and to the point. Scientists write reports using lots of big words that other scientists understand. If you use too many big words or copy ideas you don't understand, your readers won't get much out of your report. And they won't believe it really came from you.

A good report starts out by explaining what it is about and where it will take the reader. The middle part lays out your facts—what you want your reader to know about your topic. The end provides a summary of the most important things you said in your report and your most important final thought about the subject. Use this structure and your report will be a success.

Now, let's imagine that your class has been studying earth science, and your teacher asks you to spend two weeks working on a report. It should be no longer than three pages and must include graphics (pictures and charts). You decide you'd like to write something on volcanoes. Erosion takes millions of years, but volcanoes erupt—bang!—just like that.

Before you start, you need to decide whether you want to narrow down your topic. In other words, do you want to do a report on volcanoes in general, or just on one thing about volcanoes? An example of one thing is, say, the relationship between volcanoes and earthquakes. Another example could be famous volcano eruptions. As you are deciding, you might want to first see what facts and pictures are available to you.

First, let's create a file folder in our word processing program titled "volcano report" where we will store our research. Next, let's start looking for good articles, pictures, charts, and video on our subject on the Internet. Turn on your browser and type "volcanoes" into your search engine. Ours turned up hundreds of sites. One is especially kid-friendly:

Topics vs. Subtopics:
Every topic can be broken down into subtopics. For instance, pets is a big topic. But you can narrow it down by breaking it into subtopics, such as dogs, cats, birds, mice, snakes, and so on.

http://www.fema.gov/kids/volcano.htm

It has a whole page on Mount St. Helens. Also, check out the page called "Volcano Facts." If you go to it and click on "Ring of Fire," you can see the map we will be using later on.

There are sites that offer photos of volcanoes and explanations of how the shifting of Earth's surface causes volcanoes. There are also lots of color photos of volcanic eruptions. You can see right away that there are many possibilities for using text, video, audio, animation, and photos in your report. You might want to include charts, such as tables and graphs, as well.

Let's say you decide to do your report on one volcano in particular—Mount St. Helens in the state of Washington—and what caused it to erupt in 1980. Your teacher accepts the idea. The next thing to do is start planning your time.

The first thing you have to plan is how much time you want to spend on the report over the next two weeks. It's a good idea to create a real-life schedule that takes into account all of these things:

- Your access to a computer at home or school
- Other schoolwork
- Family events and responsibilities
- Extracurricular activities, such as sports and club meetings

Make a simple calendar showing your use of time over the two weeks that you have to work on your report. This may seem like extra work, but organizing time for doing work also allows you to set aside time for having fun. Include a schedule for using the school computer or going to the library to do research.

Once you've scheduled your time, you can begin creating an outline—that very useful, organized list of the different pieces of information for your report. As you create your outline and search through Web sites and books on volcanoes, keep track of your sources. A good report always includes

Kid-Friendly Site

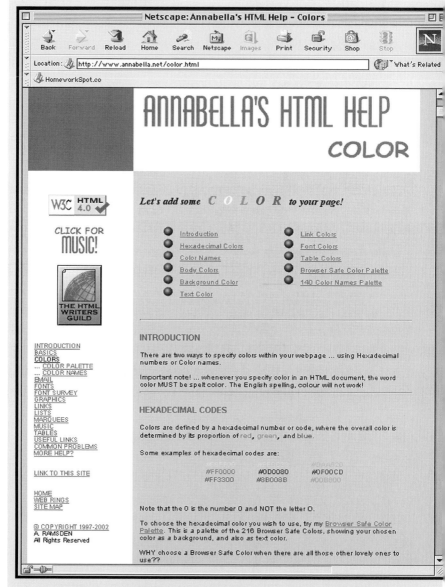

This site at www.annabella.net/netscape.html shows the 216 browser-safe colors you can use in your Web site. It also shows how they can work as either text or background colors. The site offers a great deal of useful information about the entire hexadecimal color palette.

a proper bibliography. It shows you collected information from a variety of experts, which makes your report really solid—and helps you give proper credit for other people's work or ideas.

There's one thing you'll notice about science topics. They involve a lot of jargon—the special words used in a particular field—that you'll need to explain to your Web site visitors. We're talking about terms such as *tectonic plates* and *cinder cones*. You'll need to create a glossary that is easy to use.

We've done a lot of research and are filling up our folder with pictures, graphs, and text that we can use later. By arranging all the material we are collecting, we are building an outline of our subject that is a "living document." We can change it and shuffle around topics as we discover new ideas.

With these first steps begun, we can move on to start the building process in the next chapter.

Bib- or Web- ?

Biblos is the Latin word for book. If a bibliography is a list of books used for a report, then would a list of Web site resources be called a "Web-liography"?

Chapter 2

Adding Visuals to Your Web Report

Facts are the bread and butter of your report. The text of your report must be accurate, well-organized, and interesting to read. But then there is also the visual part—the things people look at, such as pictures, maps, graphs, and other fun stuff. Using the Web, there are so many different ways to make a report exciting and interesting to the eye. You can add animation and video. You can provide links to other Web sites that show Webcasts—broadcasts and interviews about your subject matter. There are even sites with live Webcams that show visitors the most up-to-date information about your subject. (We'll show you how to do all these things later.)

With all these possibilities, choosing the best way to illustrate your topic can be a little overwhelming. A good approach is to keep a folder for visuals—either a real one or a computer file—while you are doing your research. In the folder, store Web site addresses and printouts. When you're done collecting the facts for your report, go through the folder and select the visuals that will best help you tell your story.

Before you use anything for your Web report, you have to figure out whether you need to get permission to use it. Make a list of the books and Web sites that contain the visuals you want to use, including who created them. If a company or individual operates the site, you might need written permission to use it. Sometimes, you will see it stated clearly on a Web site that the photos, graphics, or video are in the public domain. This means they are not copyrighted, and you can use them without asking permission. Government-operated sites provide pictures that are often free to use without permission. But you should give credit to the site anyway.

Always Give Credit: Even if a photo is in the "public domain," be sure to mention the photographer's name, if it's listed. Whoever took the picture should get the credit he or she deserves.

▶ Photos, Video, and Webcams

Many Web sites provide free artwork and photos that you can use. You search these sites for pictures in the same way you would search for information: Type keywords into the Search box of your browser's search engine. (If you would like more help with this, see our book *Bringing Photos, Music, and Video Into Your Web Page.*)

For our report about volcanoes, we typed the words "volcanoes, photos, free" and got quite a few results. Our favorite site was created by the U.S. Geological Survey, which is part of the U.S. govern-ment. It had lots of well-organized material about volcanoes and earthquakes. For example, on the next page are just two of the volcano photos showing Mount St. Helens before and after it erupted on May 18, 1980.

You can use these photos in your report, as long as you give written credit to the photographer. Since a government employee took the photos, our tax money has already paid for them. NASA photos and

Free Photos from U.S. Geological Survey

USGS Photo by Harry Glicken, May 17, 1980

Above is a picture of Mount St. Helens before the volcanic eruption of May 18, 1980. Below is a picture taken after the eruption.

USGS Photo by Harry Glicken, September 10, 1980

other government-owned pictures are also often free when copied from the Internet.

Video can be the best way to make your subject come alive. For some subjects, you will be able to find video on a Web site. If you have permission, you can use it in your report. You can set it up to play automatically, or, if you prefer, you can set it up to play only when the visitor clicks on an icon (picture or symbol) or a Play button and downloads it. (We'll go over this in more detail later.)

Get Permission!
Get in the habit of requesting permission to use any visuals you see on the Web. Otherwise, it's like putting your name on someone else's pictures.

Another way to use video is to include a link to another Web site that shows the video clip. Your visitors click on a button and jump over to that site. Their browser's Back button will bring them back to your site after they've looked at the video. You can also have the linked Web site's video open up in a separate window of your report. The visitor can click on a button or keyword in your text to open the window.

You should e-mail the site's creator to ask if you can include a link to the site from your report. And remember, courtesy pays! When requesting permission to use a link, photo, artwork, or video, be courteous and state your business clearly and easily. Most site managers are glad to help students.

You can also provide links to sites that have live Webcam shots of your topic or Webcast reports about it. Webcam sites have a digital camera set up that sends out live images of what it is recording. We found a Webcam site of Mount St. Helens that allows you to watch the mountain all the time (http://www.fs.fed.us./gpnf/mshnvm/volcanocam/).

▶ Maps

Maps are another great way to make complex information easy to understand for your audience. If your report is about a specific place, it makes sense to show a map of that location.

There are Web sites that allow you to download maps that you can then modify (change) to suit your needs. For example, in our report, we talk about the fact that Mount St. Helens is part of the Ring of Fire—a series of volcanoes located around the Pacific Ocean. This is a popular subject, and it was easy for us to find a map of the Ring of Fire that was free to use.

Maps Are Useful

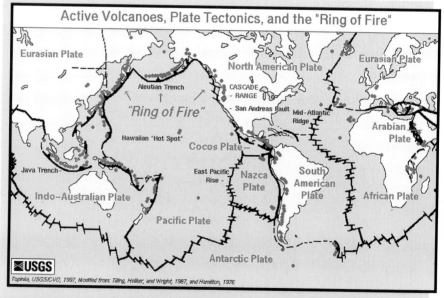

This map shows tectonic plates and the active-volcano area known as the "Ring of Fire."

There's a lot of information in this image—maybe too much. In chapter 3, we'll show you how we changed this map with a computer paint program to make it show only the information we needed.

▶ Diagrams

Diagrams are another way to explain a complicated subject. A diagram can be as simple as a couple of boxes with arrows showing step 1 and step 2. It can also be as complex as a three-dimensional model of the space shuttle. While doing research on volcanoes, we found lots of diagrams showing what lies beneath Earth's surface, all the way down to Earth's core of molten iron. Why volcanoes explode has a lot to do with what's going on beneath Earth's crust. These diagrams are very helpful.

Here's a diagram about volcanoes that we found.

Diagrams Help Explain

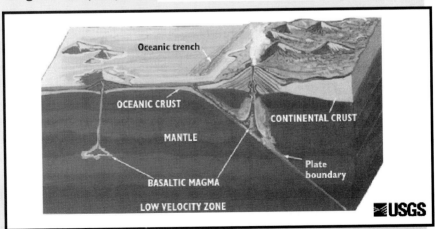

This three-dimensional diagram by the U.S. Geological Survey shows how volcanoes begin beneath Earth's crust.

If the subject of your report requires explaining

- how something is made,
- how something works, or
- a step-by-step process,

then using a diagram can be very helpful.

Copy and Trim:
If your subject is a popular one, there may be a Web site with a diagram you can use in your report. If it has too much information, try copying it and then taking out the information you don't need.

What's great about using diagrams for a Web report is that they don't have to be still images. You can animate them. For instance, you might want to have

- arrows moving across the image to show in what direction something moves,
- something changing color, or
- an object moving or changing shape right in front of your eyes.

If you can't find a good diagram on the Web, you might decide to create your own. This might be a good time to get to know your paint program and practice your computer drawing skills!

▶ Graphs and Tables

Graphs and tables are like diagrams but simpler. They allow the viewer to compare information at a glance. They offer a clear way to deliver a lot of information that involves

- quantities,
- percentages,
- statistics,
- measurements, or
- changes over time.

Graphs Can Show Changes Over Time

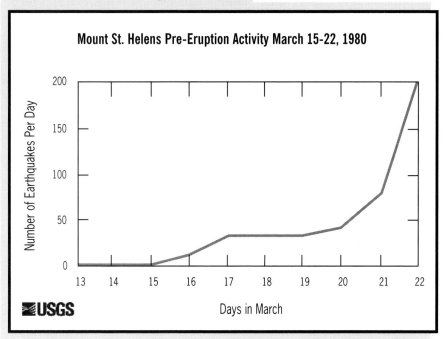

Mount St. Helens Pre-Eruption Activity March 15-22, 1980

The U.S. Geological Survey graph above shows that the number of earthquakes at Mount St. Helens went up suddenly—from 0 on March 15, to about 40 on March 17, to 200 on March 22.

The U.S. Geological Survey graph above shows the amount of earthquake activity at Mount St. Helens over a 10-day period in March, just a few weeks before it erupted. A sudden increase in the number of earthquakes that occur at a volcano site is a clue that a major eruption may occur. This graph shows that the number of earthquakes at Mount St. Helens went up dramatically between March 15 and March 22 of 1980.

Tables also compare data, but are less visual than graphs. The data is laid out in easy-to-understand boxes, or cells.

Sometimes you can create a graph using the information from a table or list. We found a lot of tables about volcanoes that listed

- different types of volcanoes,
- the most famous volcanic eruptions,
- how much matter exploded into the atmosphere,
- the strength of each explosion, and
- the number of casualties.

Tables Help You Compare

Types of Volcanoes

Volcano Type	Characteristics	Examples	Simplified Diagram
Flood or Plateau Basalt	Very liquid lava; flows very widespread; emitted from fractures	Columbia River Plateau	1 mile:
Shield Volcano	Liquid lava emitted from a central vent; large; sometimes has a collapse caldera	Larch Mountain, Mount Sylvania, Highland Butte, Hawaiian volcanoes	
Cinder Cone	Explosive liquid lava; small; emitted from a central vent; if continued long enough, may build up a shield volcano	Mount Tabor, Mount Zion, Chamberlain Hill, Pilot Butte, Lava Butte, Craters of the Moon	
Composite or Stratovolcano	More viscous lavas, much explosive (pyroclastic) debris; large, emitted from a central vent	Mount Baker, Mount Rainier, Mount St. Helens, Mount Hood, Mount Shasta	
Volcanic Dome	Very viscous lava; relatively small; can be explosive; commonly occurs adjacent to craters of composite volcanoes	Novarupta, Mount St. Helens Lava Dome, Mount Lassen, Shastina, Mono Craters	
Caldera	Very large composite volcano collapsed after an explosive period; frequently associated with plug domes	Crater Lake, Newberry, Kilauea, Long Valley, Medicine Lake, Yellowstone	

Increasing Violence
Increasing Viscosity

≋USGS

Topinka, USGS/CVO, 1997, Modified from: Allen, 1975, Volcanoes of the Portland Area, Oregon, Ore-Bin, v.37, no.9

Tables make it easy for a reader to take in a whole lot of information about a particular subject. The table above gives the basic facts about six different types of volcanoes.

Much to our surprise, we found that Mount St. Helens had a great deal of explosive power. The eruption of May 1980 was nearly as big as some of the largest eruptions in history. However, it created relatively little ash when compared to an eruption of Mount Vesuvius that heaped ash over 6 feet deep in 24 hours. In the next chapter, we'll look at how we can turn this load of ash into a graph that shows the ash getting deeper over time.

A Large Audience:
Remember, when you create Web pages for the Internet, you are actually "publishing" your report as though it were a book. The Web is public. Several thousand people might type "volcanoes, eruptions" into their search engines and come upon your site.

If your topic is a popular one, you may come across already-made tables and graphs that show the information you want to show. Again, be sure to check whether you need permission to use them.

It's time to start making our report. This is actually a lot of fun, whether it's pencil and paper, computer paint programs, or digital cameras that you have on hand. We'll learn how to translate a lot of information into pictures and diagrams that anyone

can understand. Let the creativity begin to flow!

Chapter 3

Creating Graphics for Your Report

" A picture is worth a thousand words," some wise person once said. We agree. So, let's start making pictures that tell a big story in a small space. You might want to use pictures you find on the Web, either just as they are or with some changes that you make to them. You might want to create your own pictures—drawings, photographs, or animations.

Once you have a rough sketch of the chart or illustration you want to create, you have to figure out the best way to build it. Depending on the tools available, you can construct your images any one of a few different ways. If you are drawing by hand, make your picture neat, simple, and easy to understand. If it's a chart or diagram, sketch it in pencil until it looks exactly the way you want. Then trace it onto white paper using a black marker. Make sure you print clearly and choose easy-to-see colors, such as solid reds, greens, and blues.

Once you draw your picture on paper, you'll need to make a digital version of it. One way to do this is to photograph it. If you have a digital camera, you will get to see the shot while you are taking it. The file can then be downloaded right from your camera to your computer as a JPEG file.

If you are using a film camera, tack the picture to a piece of cardboard, take it outside into the sunlight, and focus as close to it as you can (2 or 3 feet away) with the camera set on automatic. Take a few shots to be sure you get a good one. Have the film developed as a CD-ROM and choose the clearest shot. Load the JPEG picture file into the folder in which you are storing the other graphics for your report.

If you're in a hurry and your school has a print scanner, you can have one-hour prints made from your film instead of waiting for a CD-ROM. Then, ask your teacher to help you scan the print so you can load the file into your computer. Most scanners come with paint programs that allow you to crop (cut) out the things you don't want. You can brighten the picture if it's too dark and erase any unwanted marks. If your school doesn't have a scanner you can use, try your local library. You might also want to check out fast-print shops, the kind that do photocopying and other print jobs. These shops often have scanners you can pay to use. Someone there will help you make the scan.

Here's a tip. When you do scan a photo—say, a 5-by-7-inch print—into a JPEG file, make sure to scan it at its actual size. This is larger than what you'll use on your report page. But it's much easier to clean up and crop a larger picture and then shrink it down to the size you want. If you scan it in too small and then try to make it bigger, your lines will get thick and fuzzy, and the picture will look grainy.

Big to Little:
A good rule for scanning pictures is that it's always better to shrink a large file than to make a small file bigger.

▶ Tools and Techniques

Creating your own graphics using computer software allows you to type in text so it's easy to read. You can create geometric shapes with ease and experiment with different colors. It's possible to erase over and over without messing up the screen. Patterns can be made when you cut and paste the same shapes many times. There are great tools for creating diagrams, animations, graphs, maps, illustrations, and so on.

Almost all chart-making software available on the Web is complicated. Your best bet is probably just to draw a chart and scan it, or photograph it into a digital file. You can also make a chart by using your computer's paint program.

If you are going to create your graphics or change ones you found on the Web by using a paint program, then you need to understand how the Web works with colors and graphics files. You want your images to look as good as possible. You also want the file size to be as small as possible so it will load quickly onto your page. It's not hard to make both of these things happen. You just have to know a few things first.

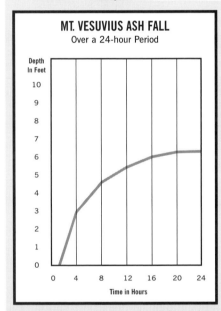

Your Own Graph

MT. VESUVIUS ASH FALL
Over a 24-hour Period

Volcanic ash graph created by the authors using a computer paint program, based on a more complicated U.S. Geological Survey chart.

▶ Small Is Beautiful

Here are some tips on making your graphic file as small as possible while you are creating it in a paint program:

Use solid lines. Clean, solid lines and solid colors take up the least amount of room. If your drawing is made of scratchy lines filled with tiny pixels or spritzed on with different colors using a paint program's Spray tool, the file size will be larger.

Use fewer colors. Sometimes GIFs are smaller if you use less color. Keep your lines clean and use blocks of solid color rather than mixed colors to save space. GIFs can only contain 256 colors. This is usually more than enough.

Lots of Colors:
Our eyes see millions of colors all the time, but our Web site colors depend on what an average computer can see. If you think 256 is not enough colors, imagine a Crayola box holding that many crayons.

▶ Palettes

When creating graphics for the Internet, you will come across something called a Web-safe palette. This is a standard set of 216 colors that Web browsers, such as Netscape, Internet Explorer, and Mosaic, share. This means that if you use these 216 colors in your artwork, then your graphic will look the same no matter what browser your visitor is using. If you use colors that are not "Web-safe," then the browser will substitute colors that are and may change the look of your graphic. This is especially true for people with computers that can display only 256 colors at one time.

You can use these colors when you create graphics in a couple of different ways. Some paint programs have a Web-safe palette of colors available to choose from. You can also download a picture of a Web-safe palette from a Web site and then use the Color Picker Tool (see the section on Paint Program Tools) to select the colors you want from that image. Some paint programs will let you convert the image you created to a Web-safe palette when you save it.

You should stick to Web-safe color values (and save the file in a GIF format) whenever you are

- using a drawing with large areas of solid color, or

- matching colors in your graphic to text colors you are using on your Web site.

If you are using photographs or complex images with lots of color, save them as JPEGs. Browsers do a good job of converting JPEG photos to images they can load.

▶ Paint Program Tools

Zap It Away!
You can draw all over a paint program screen. If you don't like what you've done, you can zap it away and start again. No paper to throw away!

To create graphics with a paint program, you need to know how to use some of the tools. Most computer operating systems come with a built-in paint program. Experiment with the tools they offer. All paint programs are fairly similar. When you open one, you are usually greeted with a blank white screen. Some paint programs come with rulers or grids, which are guidelines you can use to help you draw accurate diagrams and graphs.

Take a look at the options in the menu across the top of the screen. You can make your image larger or smaller, rotate it, flip it, and copy and paste it. You can create patterns and paint with them or fill spaces with them. Some programs have special filters that let you add effects to your drawing, such as blurring it, sharpening it, making it look grainy, or warping its shape.

One very important thing to remember when working in a paint program is to save your work every few minutes as you go along. If the computer or program shuts down for whatever reason, your unsaved work will disappear.

Here again is the map from page 16, which we have decided to modify. We think it is too big and has more details than we want to show.

Full-Size "Ring of Fire" Map

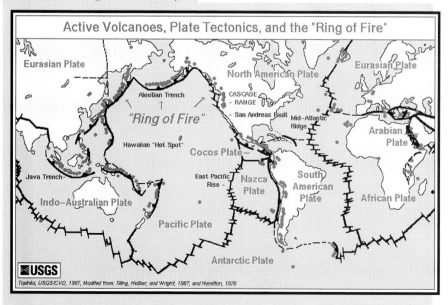

This full-size map shows more information than we need.

Here is what we did to change it.

1. First, we cropped out the part we didn't need.

2. Then, we selected the color for landmasses in the map and used it to paint over or erase the text we didn't need.

3. We emphasized the Ring of Fire by painting a fat, partially transparent black line around it.

4. Then, we placed a star over the location of Mount St. Helens.

5. Using the Line Tool, we put a border around our map.

6. Finally, we saved it.

Portion of "Ring of Fire" Map

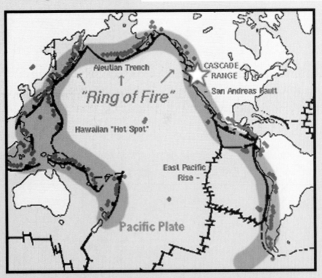

With some cropping and highlighting, we made a new map showing only the "Ring of Fire" we want for the report.

On the next page are some graphics we created in a paint program. They will be put together in an animated GIF file to show a volcano erupting.

Volcano Animation Files

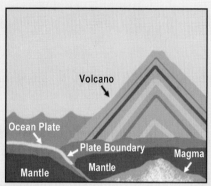

Frame 1

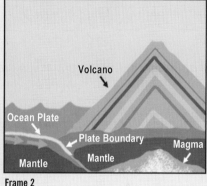

Frame 2

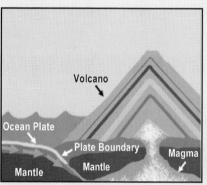

Frame 3

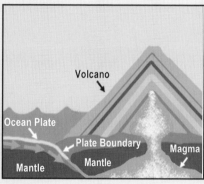

Frame 4

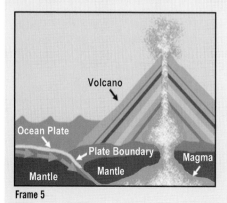

Frame 5

These five animation files show an eruption. Animation adds action to a report. You can make an animation like this with a paint program.

We created our volcano animation using the Fill Tool for the sky. We used the Paint Brush Tool and Line Tool for the mountain, mantle, and lava, and the Spray Can Tool for the magma. We used the Text Tool for the text and a Shapes Tool for the arrows. We created one arrow, copied it, changed its size and color, and rotated it for every different arrow we needed. We then saved these files as volcano_01.gif, volcano_02.gif, and so on for all five files. We animated them using a GIF construction program. (If you'd like to learn more about animation, we covered it in detail in *Creating Animation for Your Web Page.*)

▶ Saving Files

How you save your graphics file is important when creating files to be used on a Web page. Current Web browsers are able to display many different types of graphics files. Older browsers will accept only files that are saved as GIF files or JPEG files. If your image is a photograph or illustration with a lot of details, it should be saved as a JPEG. If it's a small or simple drawing, such as a chart or map, it should probably be saved as a GIF.

When naming your graphics file, keep the names short but descriptive. If the pictures go in a certain order on the page or are going to be part of an animation, end them with consecutive numbers, such as "volcano01.gif," "volcano02.gif," and so on. Use the zeroes (01, 02, 03, etc.) so that in case you get up to 11 and beyond, your files will still appear in the correct order.

When saving your files, try to keep all your letters lowercase so it's easier to type them in when you create your page in HTML. Some browsers are case-sensitive. That means that if you use a capital letter in your file name (Volcano.gif) but type in all lower-case letters when you create your page (img src="volcano.gif"), your browser won't find the file. Don't put spaces in your file name (volcano erupt.gif) or unusual characters, such as the ampersand (&).

To make it easier when it comes time to create your page in HTML, write down the file names when you create them and also write down their width and height in pixels. Each pixel is a dot of color that can be switched on or off by the computer. The picture program you use, such as Photoshop, will tell you the size of the final image in pixels. You'll need this pixel-size information when you add these files to your page.

In our next chapter, we'll get to work bringing all of our files together onto a Web page to create the report. The last step before HTML coding is to create a page layout—a plan of how all the pieces will fit together on the page.

Extensions:
Always make sure your file names have the correct extensions, such as .jpg or .gif. Make these lowercase as well. Browsers can be really fussy about that.

cat.gif
cat.tif
cat.bmp
cat.png

Chapter 4

Laying Out Your Web Report

A Web report is something really special. When you create a written report, only the people in your class will see it. But when you create a Web report, people in classes and homes all around the world can view it! You won't be there to explain to them what your report is about. You can't tell them to click on this button to see an animation or click on that link to go to the next page. Your report must be laid out so that anyone who visits your page is able to move around easily and understand what it says.

Web designers call the process of moving around a Web page *navigation*. Just as a ship captain navigates a ship using the wheel to steer, your Web site visitors navigate their way through your site with a mouse and keyboard. Navigation "buttons" allow visitors to move from page to page or to bring up special features. These buttons, which you click on with your mouse, might look like actual buttons or might instead be pictures or words in the text.

Remember how we defined *aesthetics* in the introduction to this book? It has to do with art and beauty. Your Web report is, in a way, a work of art. Whether it is good art or bad art depends on how you arrange the parts of your report on the page. It depends on the colors you choose and how welcoming your report appears to the visitor.

Your report's aesthetics are responsible for its first impression. Too many things crammed onto a page make it look crowded and difficult to navigate. Bright colors such as reds, blues, yellows, and greens banging into each other are jarring. Too much tiny text is difficult to read. Animations popping up all over the page cause confusion. A bad first impression sends visitors away, and your report goes unread.

▶ Building the Layout

We are going to design our report on volcanoes using the help of a *layout*. A layout is a rough sketch, usually drawn on paper, of the final design. This sketch allows you to shuffle parts of your report around on the page until all of them fit together nicely. You can then use the finished layout as a guide when you begin coding your report in HTML. This saves time and helps you stay organized.

Welcome!
Pleasing colors that work well together, easy-to-read text, and clear charts welcome the visitor. Your visitors will want to read what you have to say.

We'll walk you through the creation of a layout by using our report about volcanoes. As we did our research and gathered all of our photos, maps, and diagrams, we kept a list of everything we found and where we got them. The first step was to gather all of the different elements for the page. We sorted them according to the order in which we wanted to program them in HTML. We included the text, links to other sites, photos, maps, videos, and animations. Check out our list on the next page.

HOME PAGE

Title of the report

Author name(s)

Date

Text of the report (the words)

Links to other sites, Glossary, and References/Credits

Interesting Facts section

Photo of Mount St. Helens before it erupted (filename)

Photo of Mount St. Helens after it erupted (filename)

Map of the Ring of Fire

Animated GIF of exploding volcano

This seems like a pretty long list, but when you start laying it out on a page, it becomes easier to handle. If your report is more than one page long, you can create a separate list for each page. Use one sheet of paper for each page in your report. To figure out if the text will fit in the layout space, you can experiment with different text sizes and edit the words to make them fit.

To create a layout for our Web report, we used an 8½- x 11-inch piece of paper (regular notebook size). We'll show you a sample using the list above and then explain our choices.

We hand-drew our design on graph paper. Because our sample report has

Picking Paper:
If you have graph paper, use it to make your layout. It has tiny blue squares all over it. The faint blue lines will help you draw straight lines for borders and boxes.

many different parts to it, we decided that laying it out in table form would be the best approach. This way, each part can sit in its own section where the reader can find it easily. To create your layout using a computer, choose a table from your word processor's tool bar. This allows you to create boxes and move them around.

▶ Making Layout Changes

A layout, like our original outline, is a "living document." It is not carved in stone. As you think about transferring your pencil layout to the Web, you will have to make some changes. Here are some of the most common changes you may have to make.

Page Length and Width
If you find that your page is going to be long and the viewer is going to have to scroll way down, you might want to make your report two HTML Web pages. It's also a good idea to keep your Web page narrow enough so people don't have to scroll from side to side as well as top to bottom to see everything. This can be annoying.

Title Area
The title area is very important. Your title immediately tells people where they are. Word processors offer many typefaces, or fonts, from plain Arial to ZapfChancery. It's tempting to try to dress up your titles and subtitles with fancy type. The result can be confusing and hard on the eyes. Stick to type that is easy to read. One way

Page Breaks:
Pay attention to where the page breaks from page one to page two. You don't want to trim off the top of a photo or chop off the bottom of a chart.

Report Layout

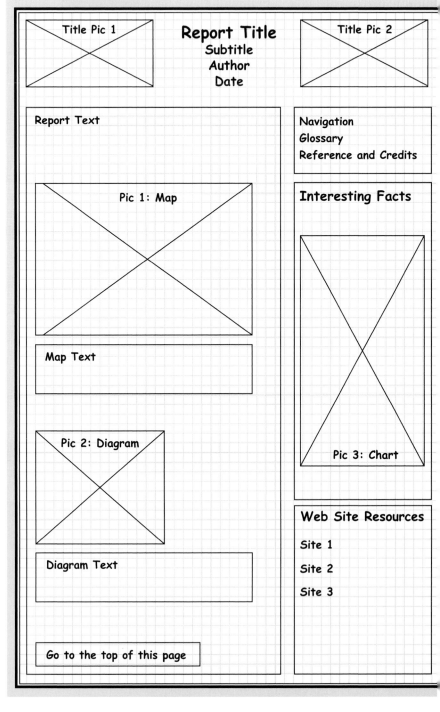

to make your title stand out is to include a small animation or a couple of pictures.

Text Area

You'll have to decide whether to place your main text to the left, in the center, or to the right on the page. The choice depends on how your text works with the illustrations you've chosen. Most people read from left to right. Text starting on the left side seems natural. But, if you have lots of charts, or features that require the reader to navigate with buttons or links to other sites, then you may want to put those important parts on the far left and the text on the right.

KIS Always:
When choosing text fonts or making other design choices, use the KIS principle: "Keep It Simple."

Navigation Links Within the Report

There are a lot of new words you will have learned after studying about volcanoes that people reading your report might not know. You might not have enough room on one page to explain all of them. A good idea is to create a "Glossary" link to a second Web page.

When the reader clicks on the "Glossary" link, a window opens to the other page, which shows a dictionary of special volcano words. When the visitor is finished looking at it, the "Glossary" window can be closed. In chapter 5, we'll show you how to do this using a PC or a Mac.

The next subtitle, "References and Credits," gets the same "invisible page" treatment. We create a page 3 that documents all our research. When the reader clicks on "References and Credits," a window opens showing a list with a scroll bar. Like the glossary page, the window can be closed with a click of the mouse.

"Interesting Facts" opens a window showing page 4. While doing our research, we learned some cool and weird things about volcanoes that we wanted to share. Since they didn't fit into the topic of our report, we put them on a separate page.

Navigation Links to Other Web Sites

A "Web Site Resources" section makes a Web report even more valuable. It leads people to other sites that offer cool things such as:

- Video of Mount St. Helens erupting, the towering ash cloud, and results of the eruption
- A live Webcam that is focused on Mount St. Helens today, including its still-smoking crater
- More charts that show the volcano's activity or the changes that happened to Mount St. Helens just before it erupted

As you can see, a lot of information about our volcano can be put into a "one-page" Web report by using links to other pages and other sites.

Read First:

When hunting for other sites to link to from your report, read each site description carefully. Some sites are really not right for kids. Check with an adult if you're not sure.

▶ Using the Layout as a Programming Guide

Your rough layout also works as a guide when you start programming. Pencil in all the details you need so they can be found quickly later. That way, when you are coding in HTML, they will be right where you want them. These details include:

- File names for the graphics (in the folder you created)
- Pixel sizes of graphics
- "Web-safe" hex-color numbers for headings, panels, and borders (see chapter 5 to learn more about hex colors)
- Text file name and location
- Fonts (type styles) you want to use for headings, subheadings, text
- Web site addresses for links

Online Updates:
A "Did You Know...?" section can list interesting facts that you can update from time to time while the report is on the Web. A related "Fact of the Day" can help bring readers back because there is always fresh information in your report.

With your layout complete, you are ready to begin coding in HTML language. In the next chapter, we'll look at each step in creating our report. We are telling a story about the Mount St. Helens volcano, but you can use our HTML code and substitute any subject you want.

We've come a long way to put everything we've learned to work in this final chapter. Now it's time to gather your layout pages, make sure all the images and text are in their folder, turn on your computer, and build your Web report.

Chapter 5

Creating Your Report in HTML

Now, how do you actually put the Web page together? We'll take you through all the code we used to create our sample report. That should give you a good idea of how to begin your own report.

First, make sure you've got everything together. You should have:

- Your layout, along with notes about sizes of art and photos, as well as lists of file names, colors, and type styles (fonts)

- The text for your report, in a word-processing document or written on paper

- A list of all of your research sources

- A list of Web sites you would like your report to link to

- A folder or directory on your hard drive with all of your graphics files in it (you'll also save your HTML files to this folder)

Let's get started. First, open up a text-editing program on your computer, such as Microsoft Notebook if you work on a PC, or a similar program if you work on a Mac. Then, open up your Web browser or whatever programs you use to view Web pages. You'll be writing HTML code in the text program and viewing the results in the browser program.

After you open a new file for your Web page in the text program, use the suffix .htm to save it as an HTML file. For example, our file will be named volcano.htm. Now open it in the browser program also. To check your work as you go along, simply save your changes in the text program. Then hit the Reload or Refresh button in the browser program to view the results.

When you build a Web site with HTML, you start at the top of the page and work your way down, line by line, using tags. A tag is any code text bracketed by arrows (< >). It helps determine how the text that comes after it will look in the browser program. The **<head>** tag introduces text that will name or describe your HTML document. Most documents add only a **<title>** tag to the head section.

Here's the title bar of our Mount St. Helens report.

Browser Title Bar

A browser reads the title of your report and puts it in the title bar. The title of this report is "Volcanoes Report."

This is the code we used:

```
<html>
<head>
<title>Volcanoes Report</title>
</head>
```

\<html> This tag tells the browser that this is an HTML document, and also creates it. The closing tag **\</html>** will come at the very end of your HTML file.

\<head>\</head> These two tags surround information that doesn't appear on the Web page itself, such as the text in the title bar.

\<title>\</title> The text you put in between these two tags appears in the title bar of your browser window. If someone has more than one window open, this can help show which window is which.

▶ Background and Text Colors

A **\<body>** tag can be used to add any background color, background properties, text, links and margin settings. We programmed the colors of our background (white) and text (black) using this code:

```
<body bgcolor="#FFFFFF"
text="#000000">
```

The F's and 0's are hexadecimal color codes.

Each color has its own code, three groups of two characters each, using numbers from 0 to 9 and letters from A to F. The "F" stands for "full" and represents white; 0 means "none" and represents black. There are 216 "safe" hex colors that will look roughly the same on all computers. You can look up the numbers of the colors at www.annabella.net/netscape.html (see page 10).

The background color is part of the **\<body>** tag. You also use the **\<body>** tag to program which colors to use for text and links. If you don't enter any color codes here, the viewer will see whatever colors are on his or her default settings. That usually means the background is white and the text black. But some people might have pink and green. Think how weird your page might look then! It's best to enter the colors you want viewers to see— even if they are black on white.

In our example above, **bgcolor** is the background color (which we've made white) and **text** is the text color (which we've made black). The colors of individual lines of text, such as titles and captions, can be made completely different colors.

You've probably come across pages that have a pattern background. You can create that by inserting an image instead of a color. If it's a small image, it can be repeated (tiled) to fill the entire background. Depending on the type of image you use, it can take a long time to load. If you decide to do this, make sure the image you are going to tile is no bigger than, say, 30 K.

The closing body tag **</body>** goes at the very end of your HTML file, right above the **</html>** tag.

Internet Addresses   Communication Facts   How Can I Be Safe?

Computer Colors

With paint, you might think of white as "no color" and black as all the colors mixed together. Computer colors are different. They represent colored light. White light contains all the colors—the full spectrum. Black is the absence of light, or no color at all. That is why the hexadecimal code for white has only F's (for "full"), while the code for black has 0's (for "none"). The rest of the hexadecimal codes represent other colors the computer can create using different combinations of colored light.

▶ Setting Up a Table

A table is a way of organizing information into boxes, or cells. The Web report page will actually be one big table. Here's the code we used:

```
<table width="590" border="0"
cellpadding="6" align="center">
```

Tables are handy tools to use in HTML to lay out where all the pieces will go in your report. An HTML table consists of rows, and you have individual cells within each row. Each cell can contain text and pictures and its own background color. The closing tag **</table>** comes at the very end of your table. If the entire Web page is a table, then the closing **</table>** tag goes above the closing **</body>** tag at the end of your HTML document.

Too Twisty:
Having to scroll from side to side and up and down is like driving a car down a twisty road. You get sick of it pretty quickly.

The first thing you need to do when creating a table is type in the tag **<table>**. Within that tag, you can set up how wide you want your table to be and sometimes how high (if you don't want it to take up the whole page). One way to do this is to use a pixel number, as in our example (**width="590"** is 590 pixels wide).

Why is the width important? Most monitors these days are set to an 800 x 600 pixel resolution. By making our table 590 pixels wide, we know that a person whose monitor is set to 800 x 600 pixels will be able to see all of our information without having to scroll from side to side as well as up and down. If the monitor is set to 640 x 480 (which is very rare), then they will have to scroll from side to side to see the whole page.

Another way to set your table size is to use a percentage number, say, **<table width="100%">**. In that case, your table would always be 100% of the screen width, or 80%, or whatever percentage you chose—no matter what the monitor is set to display. This gives you less control over what your page is going to look like on individual monitors. If the viewer's monitor is set at 1024 x 768, your table is going to stretch out to fit that size. It might look squashed, as though an elephant stomped on it.

Letting your table's cell borders show is another possible layout decision. You can even color them by using **border="insert number"**. We set our border number to **0** because we don't want borders showing on our page. We think cell borders would make the page look too busy.

Cellpadding determines how far away your pictures and text will sit from the four walls of the table cell. This allows for a nice cushion of space between pictures and text, so things aren't jammed up right next to each other. Our cellpadding is set to 6 pixels.

We wanted our table to sit centered in the browser window, so we used **align="center"**. The default setting is "flush left, left"—which means all the way to the left side of the page.

▶ Creating the First Table Row and Cells

Use the following code to start your first row:

```
<tr align="left" valign="top">
```

The **<tr>** tag tells the browser that you are working on a row. When you want to start a new row, end the row you are working on by using the closing tag **</tr>**. Start a new row simply by entering in a new **<tr>** tag.

Coding for Layout

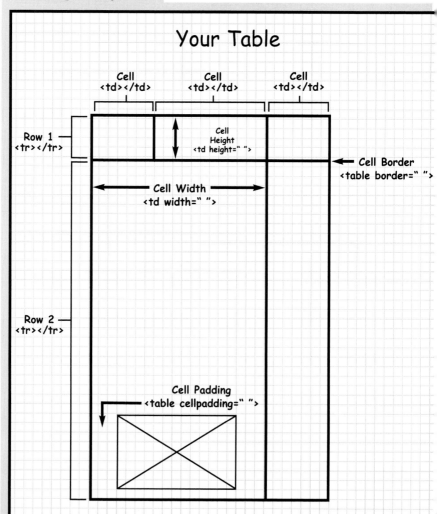

Make a sketch of your layout to see all of its parts for coding to fit the screen.

You can set the alignment—how the cells line up above and below each other—of all the cells in a row by using **align="left"** (you can select left, right, or center alignment).

Vertical alignment of text (**valign**) has to do with whether your text begins at the top, bottom, or middle of a particular cell. The default setting is "centered." If you use the code **valign="top"** your text will begin at the top of the cell instead.

The **<td>** tag defines the individual cell you are creating within a given row. You can make it a specific height and width by using **height= "number" width="number"**. When you have put everything in a cell that you want—text, pictures, an animation, or just a blank space—close the cell by typing in the closing tag **</td>**. Start the next cell by entering in a new **<td>** tag.

▶ Formatting Text in HTML

You can do a lot with text in HTML. There are many different tags that let you choose the text font you want to use, as well as the font size, color, and style (such as bold or italic).

Font Face
If your Web page is going on the Internet, a lot of people are going to be looking at it. You will want to use text fonts that are on most computers. There are three fonts common to almost every computer:

- Arial, Helvetica, sans-serif
- Times New Roman, Times, serif
- Courier New, Courier, mono

If you don't program a font, viewers will see whatever font is on their default setting. If someone has a weird font, such as Algerian, imagine what that will do to mess up your design. Take the time to specify your text font:

```
<font face="Arial, Helvetica, sans-serif">
```

Font Size and Color

You can also decide how big you want the type to be. HTML text sizes are numbered in order starting at 1, the smallest size. Number 7 is usually the largest. The heading "Volcanoes" on our page is size 6. We made it orange and bold so it stands out. (To make text bold, surround it with **<b></b>** tags.) Here's how we programmed all that information:

```
<font face= "Arial, Helvetica,sans-
serif"size="6"color="#FF3399"><b>
Volcanoes</b></font>
```

When you want to choose a new font for your next line of text or even your next word, use the closing **</font>** tag. Then type in a new tag **<font>** and list your next font. Here is the code for our subhead text "Why Mount St. Helens Erupted." We made it smaller than the other heading and colored it gray, but kept it bold:

```
<font face= "Arial, Helvetica,
sans-serif" size= "3" color=
"#666666">
<b>Why Mount St. Helens
Erupted</b></font>
```

The text of our actual report is size number 2. Number 3 is also a good size to use. Number 1 can be too small to read.

When choosing colors for your text, pick ones that are easy to read over the background you are using. Try to choose colors that fit your subject. We chose orange and dark gray for our heading because those colors are associated with volcanoes: orange fire, gray ash. We chose black for our regular text because it is easy to read.

▶ Inserting a Picture (Image) or Movie

Images

You would use a code like this to insert a picture or image into your report.

```
<img src="image_name.jpg"
width="100" height="100">
```

The **img src** tag stands for image source. It tells the HTML document where to find the image on your computer. In place of **"image-name.jpg"** just use the actual name of your image, such as "volcano01.jpg" or "erupt01.gif." You can use the **img src** tag for animated or still GIFs or for JPEG files. You must enter the pixel width and height for GIFs. You can include that information for JPEGs as well, but it's not necessary.

Your image should be in the same folder as your HTML file. If you've put it in a different folder, then you simply type

```
<img src= "folder_name/image_name.jpg"
width="100" height="100">
```

Movies

If you want your page to include a movie that has been downloaded into your file folder, use the line of code that follows but replace "movie_name.mov" with the name of your file plus the correct height and width measurements of your video window. For movies, you have to include the height and width or it won't show up on your page. This code will start the movie automatically when the visitor enters the page:

```
<embed src="movie_name.mov"
width="100" height="100">
```

QuickTime movies come with control bars for playing and stopping the movie. If you want the viewer to see those, add 16 pixels to the height of your movie window.

▶ Creating Web Links

Links Rule:

After clicking to another page, viewers can usually use their browser's Back arrow to return to page 1, but it looks better to give them a link back to the home page.

Linking to Another Page in Your Report

One of the best things about Web reports is your ability to link to other pages within the report or elsewhere on the Web. Here's how to link up with new information.

Text Link

If your report takes up two or more Web page files, you can create a link to send the viewer to a different page by using this code:

```
<a href="Page2.htm">Go to
Page 2</a>
```

Replace **"Page2.htm"** with the file name for your other page. In this example, the text **"Go to Page 2"** would appear on your Web page as the link viewers may click on. You can use whatever text you like (for instance, "Go to Glossary"), as long as viewers understand where they are going when they click on that link.

Image Link

You've probably seen Web pages where you can click on an image that links you over to another page. You can make an image a link simply by putting the **<a href>** code in front of an **img src** tag, like this:

```
<a href="AnotherPage.htm"> <img
src="image_name.gif" width="#"
height="#"></a>
```

Don't forget the closing tag **</a>** to end the **<a href>** tag, and don't forget to type in the names of your files accurately, paying close attention to spelling and capital letters.

Linking to Someone Else's Web Site

You can also use the **<a href>** tag to create a link that takes the viewer to another Web site. Make sure you type in the full Web site address:

```
<a href="http://www.website.
htm">Web Site Name</a>
```

Opening a New Window for a Link

In our report, we plan to have a glossary page. We would like our viewers to be able to look up words they don't understand. But we don't want them to have to click back and forth in the same browser window to get from one page to the next. It's easier if they can have two browser windows open at the same time. One window is for the report, the other for the glossary. All you have to do to make this happen is type the tag like this:

```
<a href="Glossary.htm"
target="_blank">Glossary</a>
```

The **target="_blank"** opens up a new browser window when the user clicks on it and, at the same time, loads the glossary page. You can use this same technique to load Web sites into their own window as well:

```
<a href="http://www.website.htm"
target="_blank">Web Site Name</a>
```

This is a good thing to use if you're not sure the Web site you're linking to will allow the user to use the browser's Back button to get back to your site.

Creating a Link Within the Same Page

We decided to provide our viewers with a link at the bottom of our long page that takes them right back to the top. This way, they don't have to scroll all the way up to get back to the beginning. To program this link, we put a target named "top" at the top of our HTML document. Here is the code for the beginning of our page again, now including the target code:

```
<html>
<head>
<title>Volcanoes Report</title>
</head>
<body bgcolor="#FFFFFF" text="#000000">
<a name="top"></a>
```

We wanted this link to the top of our page to come after the text of our report, so after the final paragraph we typed in

```
<a href="#top"><b>Go to the top of
this page</b></a>
```

The "#" symbol always sends the computer hunting for what follows it. Putting a # in front of the target name tells the browser to look for that specific target on that page.

▶ Inserting JavaScript

JavaScript added to HTML code allows the page to become more interactive, more dynamic. Some older browsers—and even some of the newest ones—don't understand JavaScript. Make sure the browser you are using is compatible.

There are Web sites that offer free samples of JavaScript code for you to cut and paste into your HTML document. Just make sure you give credit to the writer of the code, either in your Credits and References section or within the code itself by using this tag:

```
<!-- This code was written by J.
Smith. -->
```

We wanted an animated GIF in our report. We didn't want it to play annoyingly over and over again while people were reading. We also didn't want it to animate only once, because then people could miss it. We decided to set it up so viewers could roll their mouse over the GIF to watch the animation when they got to that part of the report.

This is the kind of interaction that JavaScript was made for. We found the code we needed, then cut and pasted it into the part of our HTML document where we were placing the image:

```
<a href="volcanoes_report.htm"
onMouseOver="volcano.src=
'volcanoanim.gif'"

onMouseOut="volcano.src='volcano_01
.gif'">

<img name="volcano"
src="volcano_01.gif" width=250
height=206 border=0></a>
```

Replace our file names with your own. "Volcanoes_report.htm" is the name of our main page, on which we placed our animation. If you want the animation to be a link to another page, you can use that page's Web address instead.

The GIF you want viewers to see when they roll the mouse over the image follows the **onMouseOver** tag. The **onMouseOut** tag identifies the image that will show the rest of the time, when there's no cursor rolling over it. We chose to show the first frame of our animated GIF. You'll probably want to show something for **onMouseOut**, or there will be a blank space on your Web page—and no one will know to look for an animation.

Think of "volcano" as the name of the space where **onMouseOut** leaves "volcano_01.gif," the still image of the volcano. **OnMouseOver** replaces volcano_01.gif with the file "volcanoanim.gif" instead. Either the still or the animation can occupy that space. The line "volcano.src" simply creates the space to receive either the still image or the animation.

Replace **volcano.src** with a source name that goes with your animation. If your animation is a growing flower, for example, you could call it "**flower.src**". Replace all the **.src** references with that same name.

▶ Checking Before You Go to the Web

Before you publish your Web page or present it for your class, it's a good idea to make sure the whole thing is working properly and that people can understand all the links and information. Test all the links yourself, and ask someone else to test them as well. Make sure your page looks the same on different browsers. Also double-check your text as well as any graphics or captions you wrote to make sure they are accurate. And don't forget to check your spelling and grammar, too!

Saving Face:
Proofreading and testing before you put your report on the World Wide Web could save you a World Wide Red Face later on.

We've given you quite a few tools to use for creating your Web report. You don't have to use them all. And there are quite a few more out there that haven't been covered in this book. All the tools on the Web have been designed and built by curious people like you. Keep exploring and thinking of new ways to communicate and tell your stories—and good luck on your e-report adventure.

A Simulated Web Site

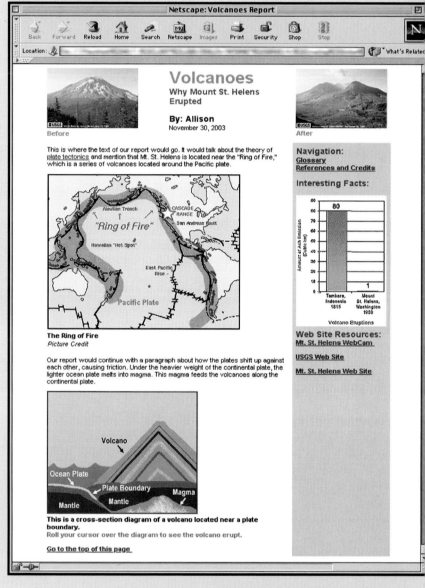

Keep in mind that any personal information you include on your Web site can be seen by everyone on the Web all over the world. If you want to be contacted, use only an e-mail address that your parents have approved. Avoid giving your full name, home address, phone number, or other identifying information.

HTML Code for Volcanoes_report.htm

```
<html>
```

Below is the text that goes in the title bar of the browser window.

```
<head>
```

```
<title>Volcanoes Report</title>
```

```
</head>
```

The body tag allows you to choose the background color and text color for your page.

```
<body bgcolor="#FFFFFF" text="#000000">
```

Below is the target for the "Go to the top of the page" link at the end of our report.

```
<a name="top"></a>
```

Now we are setting up our table along with "cellpadding" to give us some air space around our images.

```
<table width="590" border="0" cellpadding="6" align="center"
colspan="3">
```

Next comes the first row of our table.

```
<tr align="left" valign="top">
```

Next comes the first cell of our table. It contains the picture of Mount St. Helens before it exploded and the caption "Before" under the picture in orange text. The <br> tag tells the browser that the word should go on the next line—like hitting the Enter key on your keyboard.

```
<td height="122" width="151"> <img src="msh_before.jpg"
width="150" height="100">
```

```
<br>
```

```
<font face="Arial, Helvetica, sans-serif" size="2"
color="#FF3399"> <b>Before</b></font>
```

```
</td>
```

We are done with the first cell in our row and are ready for the second one. It contains the title and author of our report. Look closely. We use Arial, Helvetica, sans-serif font for all the text, but we change the color, size, and style for each line of text. Notice, also, how we use the <br> tag to control how much text we want on each line.

```
<td height="122" width="248"><font face="Arial, Helvetica,
sans-serif" size="6" color="#FF3399"><b>Volcanoes</b></font>
```

```
<br>
```

```
<font face="Arial, Helvetica, sans-serif" size="3"
color="#666666"> <b>Why Mount St. Helens Erupted</b></font>
```

```
<br>

<br>

<font face="Arial, Helvetica, sans-serif" size="3"
color="#000000"> <b>By: Allison</b></font>

<br>

<font size="2" face="Arial, Helvetica, sans-serif">November
30, 2003</font>

</td>
```

Now we are working on the third cell in the first row. It contains the picture of Mount St. Helens after it exploded and the caption "After" under it in orange text.

```
<td height="122" width="145"><img src="msh_after.jpg"
width="150" height="100">

<b><font face="Arial, Helvetica, sans-serif" size="2"
color="#FF3399">After</font></b></td>

</tr>
```

We are finished with the first row of our table, so we closed it and are starting our second row with a new <tr> tag. Since this row is only two columns instead of three, we type in colspan="2".

```
<tr>

<td align="left" valign="top" colspan="2">
```

Below is the text of our report. We are using the <p></p> tag for our paragraphs. It will automatically give us an extra line space when we end one paragraph and begin another.

We have also included a link to our Glossary page for the word "plate tectonics."

```
<p align="left"><font face="Arial, Helvetica, sans-serif"
size="2" color="#000000">

This is where the text of our report would go. It would talk
about the theory of <a href="glossary.htm#platetectonics"
target="_blank">plate tectonics</a> and mention that Mt. St.
Helens is located near the "Ring of Fire," which is a series
of volcanoes located around the Pacific plate.

</font></p>
```

Here is where we insert our image of the map of the Ring of Fire and the caption text that goes under it.

```
<p><img src="ring_of_fire.gif" width="320" height="262">

<br>

<font face="Arial, Helvetica, sans-serif" size="2"
color="#000000">

<b>The Ring of Fire</b></font>

<br>

<font face="Arial, Helvetica, sans-serif" size="2"
color="#000000">

<i>Picture Credit</i></font>

</p>
```

We've finished with the first paragraph and will now begin the next.

```
<p><font face="Arial, Helvetica, sans-serif" size="2"
color="#000000">Our report would continue with a paragraph
```

about how the plates shift up against each other, causing friction. Under the heavier weight of the continental plate, the lighter ocean plate melts into magma. This magma feeds the volcanoes along the continental plate.</font></p>

Here is the JavaScript for the animated GIF of the volcano exploding.

```
<p><a href="volcanoes_report.htm"
onMouseOver="volcano.src='volcanoanim.gif'"

onMouseOut="volcano.src='volcano_01.gif'">

<img name="volcano" src="volcano_01.gif" width=250 height=206
border=0></a>

<br>

<font face="Arial, Helvetica, sans-serif" size="2"
color="#000000">

<b>This is a cross-section diagram of a volcano located near
a plate boundary.</b></font>

<br>

<font face="Arial, Helvetica, sans-serif" size="2"
color="#CC6600">

<b>Roll your cursor over the diagram to see the volcano
erupt.</b></font></p>
```

Here is the link that takes viewers to the top of the page. We will also finish this cell of row two with the </td> code.

```
<p><font face="Arial, Helvetica, sans-serif" size="2"
color="#000000"> <a href="#top">

<b>Go to the top of this page </b></a></font></p>

</td>
```

This is the code for the second cell in this row, which will contain our Interesting Facts and our links to other pages.

```
<td width="145" valign="top" bgcolor="#FFCC99" align="left">

<p><font face="Arial, Helvetica, sans-serif" size="3"
color="#993300">

<b>Navigation:</b></font>

<br>
```

This is the link to the Glossary page. It also opens up a separate browser window for the page. Remember, the code here only establishes a link to the glossary page. The actual glossary page would still need to be created, using the same kind of coding used to create this main report page.

```
<font face="Arial, Helvetica, sans-serif" size="2"
color="#666666">

<a href="glossary.htm" target="_blank">

<b>Glossary</b></a></font>

<br>
```

This is the link to the References and Credits page.

```
<font face="Arial, Helvetica, sans-serif" size="2"
color="#666666">

<a href="reference.htm" target="_blank">
```

```
<b>References and Credits</b></a></font></p>
```

This is the text for the Interesting Facts section, with our chart inserted as well.

```
<p><font face="Arial, Helvetica, sans-serif" size="3"
color="#993300">
<b>Interesting Facts:</b></font>
<br>
<p><img src="ash_chart.gif" width="145" height="215"></p>
<p><font face="Arial, Helvetica, sans-serif" size="2"
color="#666666">
</p>
```

This is the text for the Web Site Resources section with our links to other Web sites.

```
<p><font face="Arial, Helvetica, sans-serif" size="3"
color="#993300">
<b>Web Site Resources:</b></font>
<br>
<font face="Arial, Helvetica, sans-serif" font size="2"
color="#666666">
<a href="http://www.fs.fed.us./gpnf/mshnvm/volcanocam/">
<b>Mt. St. Helens WebCam </b></a></font>
<br>
<br>
<font face="Arial, Helvetica, sans-serif" font size="2"
color="#666666">
<a href="http://vulcan.wr.usgs.gov/">
<b>USGS Web Site</b></a></font>
<br>
<br>
<font face="Arial, Helvetica, sans-serif" font size="2"
color="#666666">
<a href="http://vulcan.wr.usgs.gov/Volcanoes/Cascades/
volcanoes_cascade_range.html#msh/">
<b>Mt. St. Helens Web Site</b></a></font></p>
```

Now we are done with this cell, and with this row and with this table and with this Web page! Here are all our closing tags.

```
</td>
</tr>
</table>
</body>
</html>
```

Glossary

copyright—The legal protection of ownership. For example, if a photographer copyrights his or her photographs with the U.S. Copyright Office, then no one can use the photos without the photographer's permission.

JavaScript—A Java-coded program that may be typed directly into an HTML-coded program to create a special effect. The JavaScript code can be seen and changed if needed, unlike the hidden code in a Java applet.

keywords—Words that, when typed into a browser search engine, lead to other Web sites. Typing "volcanoes, eruptions" into a browser search engine will produce a list of other Web sites that mention these topics.

links—Lines of code that allow a visitor to a Web site to switch back and forth between pages in the site, or to other Web sites. It's good Web design to provide a return link to wherever the visitor started, if possible.

navigation—Moving among the different elements of a Web page, as well as moving from place to place by rolling the mouse cursor over an image or a line of text. The site designer should make the Web site easy to navigate.

paint program—Any software program used to create or manipulate graphics. The paint programs that come with most computer operating systems are simple, but there are also more sophisticated programs, such as Photoshop.

pixels—Short for "picture elements," the basic units of color that can be programmed on a computer display or in a computer image. Image sizes are measured in pixels.

plug-ins—Software programs that can display special effects or play audio and video files. Most can be downloaded for free and "plugged into" a Web browser.

print scanner—A device that allows anything flat, such as text pages or photographs, to be laid on its glass surface and scanned with a moving light wand to create a computer file. Many scanners allow cropping and sizing of the scanned image.

rollover—An effect that is activated when the visitor moves the computer cursor over that part of the Web page. For example, when the cursor moves over Jane's picture, Jane's voice says, "Hello."

video clip—A short video program. A video clip might last only a few seconds.

Further Reading

Basch, Reva, and Mary Ellen Bates. *Researching Online for Dummies*. Foster City, CA: IDG Books Worldwide, 2000.

Branscomb, H. Eric. *Casting Your Net: A Student's Guide to Research on the Internet*. Boston: Allyn & Bacon, 2001.

Dawson, Dennis, and Mark Kistler. *Mark Kistler's Web Wizards*. New York: Fireside, 2000.

Flynn, Mike. *Inside a Web Site*. Danbury, CT: Grolier Educational, 2001.

Lindsay, Bruce, and Dave Lindsay. *Dave's Quick 'n' Easy Web Pages*. Calgary: Erin Publications, 1999.

Index